# Clint Faraday
book 59
*Dead Giveaway*

"Clint? Amanda Presley here. I met you in David, two months ago? You said to call if there were any problems about the place I bought?

"Well, I'm not sure if it's a scam, or not, but they want me to sign a thing in Spanish, and I only have what they said it says. Does that sound like it could be a scam?"

"It sounds like a dead giveaway. Tell them to kiss your ass!"

They made a plan.

Then her brother and ex-husband ended up dead. Why them? Why not Amanda? Everything was in her name.

# Contents

# About the author

CD Moulton has traveled extensively over much of the world both in the music business, where he was a rock guitarist, songwriter and arranger and in an import/export business. He has been everything from a bar owner to auto salvage (junkyard) manager, longshoreman to high steel worker, orchid grower to landscaper, tropical fish farmer to commercial fisherman. He started writing books in 1983 and has published more than 350 books as of January 1, 2023. His most popular books to date are about research with orchids, though much of his science fiction and fantasy work has proven popular. He wrote the CD Grimes, PI series, and the Det. Nick Storie series, Clint Faraday series, and many other works.

He now resides in Gualaca, Chiriqui, Panamá, where he writes  books, plays music with friends, does research with orchids and medicinal plants. He has lately become involved in fighting for the rights of the indigenous people, who are among his closest friends, and in fighting the extreme corruption in the courts and police in Panamá.

He offers the free e-book, *Fading Paradise*, that explains what he has been through because of the corruption.

CD is the discoverer of the Chadam Protocol for curing cancer.

Facebook page Ambrosia peruviana for cancer.

# Dead Giveaway

## *Amanda Calls*

Clint Faraday, PI, retired, now declared Ngobe Indio, watched as his son, Nito, went along the white beach toward the little town of Cusapín, and sighed. He was seventy five, going on fifty, had the best wife and family in the world, was enjoying exceptionally good health, was a multi-millionaire, and was living in paradise.

Clint looked like he was about fifty. Tyna, his beautiful, wife was fifty, but looked like about thirty five. His daughter was a medical doctor and medicinal plant expert, and his son was a criminologist with the highest scores in his graduating class at UP. He was now a doctor of sciences, with a degree in forensics sciences.

Clint had raised his children in the Indio tradition. That it was a far superior way was obvious, particularly when they were around most others their age who were raised in the cultures of the socalled "civilized" world. He was damned proud of them, and didn't care who knew it!

He would help with the rice, today. He had helped prepare the large area where it was grown, and had put in the irrigation from the little lake higher in the mountains. The stream ran right against the field. It was a matter of leveling the area and getting all the surface rock out. No easy task!

Four years now, they raised all the rice the Eastern fourth of the comarca needed. It was just harvested and dried. He would help with the removing of the harder husks. Most people preferred, as did he, the whole grain.

Clint was a multimillionaire, due to no fault of his own, but still conducted himself like any other Ngobe. He had a place in the community, where he belonged. Gringos were usually flabberghasted when a millionaire was doing the backbreaking work of people he could hire a crew to replace.

He belonged. Here, he was part of a community, not someone who lived in it. He had a place. None of them did. He was content. None of them were. He was a rarity, because he had a lot of money, it didn't have him.

He was also in better shape, at seventy five, than any of them were at thirty.

Naldo, a neighbor, came to say they wouldn't dehusk rice, today. The fog didn't let it dry quite enough. They would do it tomorrow.

So. He would work in his own garden.

His cellular buzzed. That was the only real

thing he had from the outside that he used.

"Clint? Amanda Presley here. I met you in David, two months ago? You said to call if there were any problems about the place I bought?

"Well, I'm not sure if it's a scam or not, but they want me to sign a thing in Spanish, and I only have what they said it says. Does that sound like it could be a scam?"

"It sounds like a dead giveaway. Tell them to kiss your ass!"

"Dead giveaway?"

"It's fraud, by definition, if you don't also have a translation into English. It's obviously a scam, of some kind.

"What is it they want you to sign?"

"Something called a trespass, or something. They say it's a permit for someone to cross my land. They won't be trespassing. It's like a permission for them to be there, and to bring other people there. It's to be only in Quita Santana's name, so she would have to be with whoever."

"A traspas is the same as a title, almost. It would put the land in Santana's name.

"Amanda, I'll get in touch with a friend in Panamá City who has a connection with the courts. He's, as is unusual here, not corrupt. Maybe he can get you in with the anticorruption board. They can use this to get rid of a few of those type – if you agree, of course."

"I more than agree. I'd start something like that, myself! Go for it! Maybe their dead give-away would leave their little scam dead in the water, so to speak. I can use a little excitement in my life!"

"It could get very damned dangerous. I won't try to kid you about that!"

"All the better! I never planned to live forever anyhow!"

"Rojelio Armands will be in touch, very soon. We have to act before they figure you've caught on. Try to stall them a little. Gain some time. Tell them you have to go somewhere, for a few days, or something."

"Done!"

"Oh! Where are you? Bocas?"

"No. Punta Peña. You may know them from Bocas though. That's where they're from. Relio Portas and Berto Jailisco. Quita is Berto's wife, or significant other, or whatever they call it, here."

"I've met them. There was a lot of crap a close friend went through because of them."

"Well, they said they were working with an old man who's sort of a legend. He's in Costa Rica, or somewhere, but they say he would definitely recommend them. They say that he has to be two hundred years old. Their parents knew him when he was already old enough to retire here."

"They give a name?"

"Dave something."

"Dave? He's in Gualaca, right now. He's the one they caused the trouble. He would recommend them like he would recommend cancer. He's about ninety two, I think. Tell you what! Tell them you have a friend who got in touch with Dave. You plan on going to David tomorrow, anyhow. You can stop in Gualaca to have a talk with him. Do they want to come along?"

She laughed. "That will light a fire under their asses! I have to go to David to meet with my brother and my ex. They're here on business. They have some land deal, too. Supposed to be next week, but I can make it now."

"Just be sure you're somewhere they can't reach you when you tell them the good news."

"D'ju godt it!"

"Your ex is still a friend?"

"Oh, certainly! The breakup was about the fact he as much as worships money. We were never what you could call 'in love,' or anything. He chases money to the point he takes wild get-rich-quick chances, then I had to bail him out. The business was always mine. He hit one scheme, and wanted to force me out. I dumped him when our son, Richard, was eighteen. Ricky left to get away from the shady deals and big gambles. He's in California, doing very well, without the distratcions. He's not like his father, where money's concerned. It's more a sort of gambling addiction, with George, I think."

"Well, be damned careful around these types."

"That's a promise!"

"Clint? Amanda. I'm on a bus on my way to David. I don't want to be a constant bother, but a young man from Bocas was at the restaurant when I got on the bus. He got on, too. I saw him talking with the Relio character, several times. They didn't know I saw them. Once in Bocas, and once in Chiriqui Grande, then once in Punta Peña.

"The man's name is John, I think."

"Black. Fairly handsome. Sort of hoody acting?!

"Dead accurate! Sort of an 'I'm better than you' attitude."

"Watch him. He works for Relio, a lot of the time. He would be a hit man if he actually had the guts he tries to make you think he has. He's a real bad-ass – so long as he's with two or three buddies."

"It would be fun if I get off in Gualaca, hmm?"

"Be careful! It's no game!"

"Gualaca is that pretty little clean town, just as you get off the mountains, isn't it?"

"Uh-huh."

"I'll get off at the big China, and see if he does

the same."

"He'll go a little farther, probably to the bombas, just two blocks farther, and walk back. Dave has a place down the road, just west of the China. He'll assume you're going there. When he goes on, take the road to the east of the China, and go the four blocks to the park. The Gualaca bus for David leaves from there every half hour. If he sees you getting on that bus, he dares not take it. He'll have to wait for the next one. You're in David in forty minutes, and can be where he can't find you.

"I think ... why not go the block past the park? The police station is there. People will tell him you went that way. The cops there know me. Talk to Quintero, if he's there. You can be on the porch when John comes looking for you. Tell Tero I told you to report him. Let him see you identified him to the police. Tell Tero you think he's following you. That's why you went to the estacion. You don't know what it's about, but you are in a deal concerning land purchases, and he was seen talking to Relio, several times, but they didn't seem to want you to know they even knew each other.

"Tero knows all about that bunch!

"Tero knows Dave. He'll know if he's in town. If so, go spend a half hour or so at his place. Tell him about it. He'll put a burr or two under that whole bunches saddles!

Amanda giggled, and said she'd stay among as many people as she could manage. They could see what happened. She would go on into David, later, and surprise her ex and her brother. They didn't know she was coming.

Clint warned her, again. She would call him, later, to let him know what happened in the interim.


"Clint? Amanda. I just got into David. It was more of a surprise to my ex and brother than I expected. They would have gotten the whores out of their rooms, if they expected me. It was sort of fun. I told George we're divorced, and my brother, Ethan, could use a little female companionship. He already has a few more gay tendencies than a lot of people.

"I don't think he's gay, but he says and does things that seem to point to tendencies.

"Anyhow, they managed to get rid of me, for a couple of hours. Business, you know, Old Sock.

"I told them I couldn't care less. I have a couple of boyfriends, myself. Ethan was totally shocked, not that I had boyfriends, but that I'd say so in front of my own brother!

"I said my ex tried to hide his girlfriends from me for all the years we were married. He knew about a couple of them. Where does he get off thinking it was okay for Hubby-dear, but wifey was supposed to be absolutely celibate, if Hubby-dear wasn't there.

"Sudden case of the stutters. George couldn't believe I knew about any of that. He thought I would bring it up at the divorce, if I did. I told him I had enough, without that! Why cause a lot of grief, when it wasn't necessary?

"We're to meet at a large property near Dolega, in the morning. He has some things he wants to discuss. We have a chance to make a killing, for very little investment – like I haven't heard that, before!

"Sorry. I don't mean to unload on you. You couldn't care less.

"That John character did exactly what you said. I was standing out front of the police station, with Tero – who's a very nice person – and he came around the corner and almost ran into us. Tero asked why he was following me. We got the old 'Who? Me?' act. It really shook the ass up. He was on the phone, talking with someone when he walked away. I could hear something about it being some kind of a trap.

"Oh! Dave was in the mountains. I may have seen him when we passed, in the bus. The driver honked at an old man, up there. Said he was a real character. Ninety years old, and still wandering in the mountains, all by himself,

taking pictures of plants, and collecting a few –
and aluminum cans! Is that him?"

"Yep! He says picking them up takes a little of
the garbage out of the road, and he can make the
bus fare up there. They're just laying there. Why
not?"

"Well, I'll let you know if there's anything *to*
let you know."

"Fair enough. Be careful."


It was a beautiful morning in a place where
almost all of them are. Clint watched the
sunrise, with his coffee, then told Tyna he was
going to be processing the rice, today. She said
the women were going to be shelling beans and
peas, most of the day. Berto and Andres would
take the produce to Chiriqui Grande, tomorrow
morning, to sell. They would bring back flour
and some things people needed. They would
like for Clint to burn off the cashews, tomorrow,
so don't plan anything else.

Clint had studied the way cashews were
handled, and had set up a bit of a very profitable
business with them. They were all over the
place. He also had a deal with almonds, which
were also everywhere you went. He designed a
cracker to get the almonds out of the tough
husks. Cashews were still handled by hand. He
had made the process as safe as he could.

(The cashew has a highly caustic oil in the shell that has to be burned off. There was still a bit of it when the husks were removed. People had to be careful to wear latex gloves when handling them. The residual oil was evaporated, after the husks were removed. That roasting process was with butter, to give the cashews the flavor and texture that made them so delicious.)

About 9:30, Clint's phone buzzed.

"Clint? Amanda. I'm at the property. George and Ethan are here. They're dead!

"I need advice."

"How did you get there?"

"I have a rented car."

"How were they killed?"

"I think they were shot. George is under some trees, not far into the place. Ethan is about a hundred meters farther. They're both on the road through the middle of the place.

"Clint, George said they would be with the people who were handling the sale, so I could ask them whatever questions I liked. I would see how this was a no-miss deal.

"I wonder if just maybe pulling that act in Gualaca is behind it, but I can't say how or why."

"Okay. Call the police, and wait for them. I'll come there, if there's no other way. Do *not* be alone anywhere near any of the people behind the deal.

"I assume there's no car your brother and ex went there in?"

"No. Only mine, but that ... I see! They were coming out here with those people to show me the land! Where are those people? It almost has to be them who killed George and Ethan, doesn't it? They would have to be dead, too, or would have reported the killings, themselves. I don't see any other way it could be."

"We can hope they didn't think about that, before. Call the police. Change that part about waiting for them. Get out of there! You're the only one, so far as they know, who could say your ex and brother went out there with them."

"Oh, God! A car's coming!"

"Are you near your car?"

"I'm in it!"

"Get out of there! Now!"

"Roger!"

There was a short delay, then she said she had turned around, and was at the main road. She would call the police. She would tell them the whole story.

"No! Call them, and report going out there and finding the bodies, and that you ran when a car came in. It's private property, isn't it?"

"Yes. That would scare the piss out of a poor helpless woman. I panicked and ran."

"Don't give them your name, when you call. Go to Gualaca, and tell Tero the whole thing. He can help you with the David police. I know Tero's not corrupt. Too many in David are."

"I don't...?"

"Those people would pay someone off to not find any evidence."

"I heard Chiriqui was like that. Okay. I know this road, pretty well, for a stretch. This car's just like a lot of others. I don't think they followed me out. They aren't chasing me. I wonder why?"

"Because they went out there to meet some people, and found them dead. There was a car that fits the one you're driving. Perfectly. They probably can even give the license number. Get to Tero!"

"I had an experience, in the states ... I can turn that back on them!"

"This isn't a game!"

"I guaran-fucking-tee you I know that little fact! I'm going to leave them a huge question to answer! A *huge* question!

"Listen, Clint. You don't have to get too wrapped up in this mess. I'll call you and keep you up to the minute, but I have a few little tricks, of my own. Don't come running here, unless I really need you to. There's no way they saw for certain it was me driving this car."

"Don't set something up that can come back to smack you in the puss!"

"I won't. I see something I really need. Talk later!" She rang off.

Clint shook his head. This could get damned serious, if Amanda didn't get out of her fantasy land. That bunch would kill her as quickly as they killed her husband and brother.

He couldn't do much of anything, but he did call Tero to ask that he help Amanda, any way he could. Tero said he was afraid there would be trouble, but he didn't expect it to include murder. He would do everything he could. Clint explained that the people who did this would probably identify Amanda's car as having been there.

"Yes. They will report going there to meet with Mr. Presley, and found him and the brother there, dead. Mrs. Presley was seen speeding away in her rented car. Thus, when she reports the deaths she will have a suspicion in place. Her testimony that the dead men went there with those people will be questionable."

"But she did report it. To you, the policeman who confronted one of them in Gualaca. You're the only one she could trust, owing to Chiriqui's reputation of corruption."

"We will most certainly use that point, in her defense!"

"She plans something. Try to stop her from getting into a situation she can't get back out of. I think she's in some TV fantasy world, where she can outsmart those hoods."

"From my talking with her, yesterday, it would not surprise me if she was able to do something. The lady is very intelligent, and has a very unpredictable personality. I think she would not do anything that could lead to complications, in such a matter. She is resourceful, I truly think.

"She did use an expression you taught to me. 'Fight fire with fire.' Possibly, she has thought of some way to set a backfire, do you suppose?"

"It wouldn't surprise me!"

Clint rung off, and thought, for a minute. He wondered what Amanda was going to try. He did think, from what he knew about her, she had the brains to be able to put an obstacle or three in the way of that wad of amateur wanabes.

He went back to the rice. All he could do was wait.


"Clint? Amanda. I'm under arrest, and on my way to David. Tero is going with me. He'll drive my rented car in for me. He says they don't have enough to more than make me fill out a bunch of testimony forms. It's sort of exciting, in a negative kind of way. Oh! I see those people did exactly what I thought they'd do. What you said.

"Poor little old me! They won't even tell me what it's about. All they said was that my car was reported being seen at a crime scene. They didn't even tell me what kind of crime! It's not even my car! It's one I rented. Do you think maybe the one who had it before did something?"

"I can take it Tero didn't tell them anything, and that there's someone there you believe can speak English?"

"Yes! Exactly! It doesn't even make any sense. My car couldn't have been seen anywhere near a crime scene!

"Well, it could. I was at the Chiriqui Mall. Maybe, if there was a holdup, or something. That would mean there were a hundred cars seen there. I don't know. I went from there to Gualaca to try to talk to that Dave person you were telling me about. I stopped and talked to Tero – he's the policeman I talked to yesterday, when I felt I was being stalked – and he got a call, and had to hold me and take me to David. He says he wonders how anyone knew I was in Gualaca. He said that was a suspicious piece of data to consider.

"Do you think I should get a lawyer? I mean, I haven't done anything, but I don't know how that works, here. I know you would be able to recommend someone. The only lawyers I know are with land sales, and like that.

"What now?" Clint heard someone say she wasn't supposed to be talking on a phone until the captain said she could, and he could get in trouble. "Oh, sorry! I'll talk later, Clint! Bye!" She rang off.

Why in hell did she sound so happy?

Clint grinned. She would be the dingbat who found an adventure in such things. It wouldn't ever occur to her that this was a serious matter. She called her friends and told them about how exciting it was!

That she had something set up was beyond question, but what was it?

Another thing occurred to him. She could have actually done it. This was all playacting to get him to have her get away with it. He still had the reputation with the police of solving crimes. He had very seldom represented a guilty party, but that did happen, a time or two.

A couple of times in twenty five years was a pretty solid record.

He didn't hear anything else for more than four hours.

"Hi, Clint! My little adventure was a lot more serious than I ever thought! There were two people *murdered*, and they thought I was there, because my car was reported as being there.

Somebody anonymous got the license number, can you believe?

"Well, anyway. I got taken all the way to the Ciudad Judicial, and they, I guess what you'd call 'grilled' me, for more than an hour when somebody was sent out to check over my car for a weapon, or something. The woman came in, and went to whisper something to that Ramos asshole, who was treating me like a piece of dogshit on his shoe. She said something, and he went out with her, then they came back, and said it was all a mistake, and, ha-ha, these things happen.

"I mean, drag me all the way down here, and just laugh and say it was a mistake? I was under arrest! Isn't that, like back home, a false arrest? Can I bring charges?

"I mean, I would never do that, except Ramos spent hours being a total asshole! Then he laughs it off, and says it's a mistake? A mistake they could have found back in Gualaca, if they'd checked whatever it was they checked on my car?

"Okay. I'm out front now. They can't hear me. Exactly what you said happened. Somebody took down my license number, out there, supposedly. Anonymous, and they pull this shit?

"This means it has to be Relio and that bunch, doesn't it?"

"That's too obvious to miss. What happened about the car?"

"Oh, that. The license number wasn't what was on my car. They checked with the rental company to find me, but they never have explained why they knew I was in Gualaca. Nobody ... he's coming back (whispered) ... bothered to even check that? I mean, wouldn't you check, the first thing, to see if it was even the right car? I mean, a whole *day* wasted with this bullshit routine, and it wasn't even the same car they could have checked in Gualaca? I can't do anything about it?"

"Their setup failed. They'll have to come after you. You have to disappear. Do you have a way?"

"Well, I can, if I really have to. I just don't see how they can be so damned stupid! Whoever made the anonymous call had to be the one who did whatever, killed them, or whatever. I'm not the brightest candle on the cake, but I can sure enough see *that*!

"I wonder who the dead people are. They never even told me that! That asshole kept asking if I knew the older one, or the younger one, and that kind of thing, but I don't even know who was killed! I mean, give me a damned *break,* already! This is pure *horseshit*!

"Here's Tero. He's a real prince! He's the only

decent one in this bunch! Maybe he can tell you something.”

“Ah, Mr. Faraday? It would seem we have another strange case! I have to get back to Gualaca. Mrs Presley has kindly offered to drive me, there. Perhaps I will contact you, later.

“Mrs Presley says she doesn’t even know who was killed. I would think they would have informed her. It was her own brother and ex-husband!

“Mrs Presley! What...? Oh, how thoughtless of me! I’ll talk later. Mrs Presley was shocked, terribly, when I said that!” he rang off.

Clint grinned. Tero would help her with that act. He was after that bunch in the fiscalia as much as he would be after Relio and company. This couldn’t be hidden nearly so easily as things in the past. Amanda had come through, there! Ramos had his crooked ass in a crack. He would have to come up with an explanation for things he no longer had an explanation for.

Clint thought, for a few minutes. He would do the cashew burn tomorrow morning, then could be in David, just after dark. Maybe he finally had the kind of break he could use to help Tero tag that bunch of crooks, both in and out of the police and court system.

"It would seem as though Amanda is a bit brighter than our erstwhile Inspector Ramos," Tero said, with a smirk. "You would have been most amused with the way she had him thinking she was totally lacking in mental facilities.

She told me exactly what happened. She explained what she had done, and stated her reasons, quite well. She decided that there was only one possibility as to who killed her ex-spouse and her brother. She could see the setup. She exchanged the license plate on her car for that on a much older car that was the same color. It was outside of a workers' pension. The owner was, most probably, at work, some-where."

Clint nodded. "But can you be absolutely certain that's the only explanation, here?"

"Personally, yes. Professionally, I am forced to consider that she could be the guilty party, and is using what has happened to her elsewhere to cover the fact."

Clint nodded, again. "Exactly the same here. What convinces me she isn't the killer is the ones she's become involved with over that land.

"I'm assuming it was that land?"

"No, I don't think so. It doesn't seem likely. That is the one consideration that gives me a slight pause."

"Now we have a real problem! If it isn't the same property, with the same people, who else is in.... It doesn't make any sense!

"Okay. That old bunch of crooks are almost my age, give or take twenty years. They've gotten away with stealing the retirement of a number of people, over the past thirty years. The police and courts are used, in Chiriqui, mostly, because they're known to be totally corrupt. That explains Amanda's involvement. She's here to buy property. They moved right in.

"We have to know everything about that property. I think it'll be something they've stolen from some retiree. They suddenly have reason to think maybe Amanda's working with the corruption board, in Panamá City. Amanda was coming to David with that – so where in hell does her ex-husband and brother fit into that?

"The ex and her brother are also looking for investment property. She was to meet with them. They end up dead, in a setup that would leave Amanda in deep shit for an explanation of any of this.

"It still doesn't make sense! They would be

trying to kill Amanda, not her ex and brother!"

"I intend to do a bit of investigation about that land, here. Who owns it? Is the owner the seller?

"Clint, it still doesn't make sense. This was set up to get rid of the ex-husband and brother, and to leave Amanda a tainted witness against them for the land fraud, due to the fact she was under suspicion of murder. Ramos et al could claim there was no evidence to investigate, other than the anonymous tip about her being seen racing away from the murder scene. That explains what happened here, but does nothing to explain ... it still doesn't make sense, unless I find the same people were involved in the land deal, here. They would then assume the ex-husband and brother were working with Mrs. Presley to expose them to the corruption board.

"Clint. That is the *only* way it would make any sense!"

"I agree. I think just maybe ... Tero, the ex was into shady deals. Do you think it's possible he was doing the setup of Amanda, for some reason?

"See if he came here before her! Find out if he had contact with Relio and company! I see *one* way it makes sense!"

"I see. Then the deaths of the ex-husband and brother would be an example of what you term 'poetic justice' – wouldn't it?"

"I had a case where a woman hired a hit man to get rid of a husband. She had it set up so a couple of people would end up dead, and their insurance would finance everything else. The people to be hit weren't at the place they were supposed to be met – but she was! All the hit man knew was that he was to hit the people in a grey rented Honda, then she would meet him in David with the money, or arrange for him to get it without her ever knowing who he was..

"She was also driving a rented grey Honda. The money was in a sack, in the back seat. She didn't speak enough Spanish to stop him. In effect, she paid for her own hit."

"Something very much like that could have happened here.

"I still wish to do something about the corruption that was part of the plan."

"I'm with you, all the way. I'm here, anyhow. Let's see what we can do. It'll solve this case, as a bonus!"

They shook hands.


"We will have to give a better description of George Presley and Ethan Fields," Tero announced. "It seems rather possible they were in Bocas three weeks before Amanda arrived."

"I talked with Amanda, this morning. She says they might have been, but they never told her anything about it. All she knew was that a business acquaintance told her about the place in Bocas, so she came to look at it. She had been to Panamá, twice before, and was considering having a six months place, here. She then looked very thoughtful. She has it figured that they were trying to set her up, somehow. It was plain on her face."

"I have arranged with the registro to search about the properties, both that Mrs. Presley was discussing and that the ex-husband was interested in. I will have to use the police computer. A secretary in David is seeking the information. I know her well. She will not allow anyone else to know what she's doing. She is one who helps me with the investigation of the fiscalia, there. I will go to great extremes to protect her."

"Fair enough. Amanda said they wanted to go into a partnership with someone to build a hotel and exclusive casino and golf course on the property they were after. They were into shady deals. What she told me sounds like a money laundering deal. She wouldn't put that past them, for a picosecond."

"Hmm. And our other suspects are looking for a way to finance their own retirements. Rather likely, wouldn't you say?"

"I'd say something almost exactly like that."

There was some noise from the front. Dave, the old man they had talked about, yesterday, with Amanda, came in to greet Clint.

"You here to look for the ones who tried to kill me yesterday, in the mountains?" he asked.

"Someone tried to kill you!?" Tero cried.

"Don't get excited. It's a long way from the first time. I saw that car almost run off the road as the passed me, then it started backing up. I got behind some crap, and they fired about twenty rounds into the bushes I was in when they passed.

"Black two oh eleven Mitsubishi SUV. Costa Rican plates. There was a 'D' on it. I couldn't see more, except for a black scumbag from Bocas known as Big Bad John was driving, I think. It wasn't the driver who shot. I couldn't see who that was. I can guess, within a very damned few.

"Juanito said they found two dead bodies over in Dolega that were connected with the gringa who was here, yesterday. You're here today. One and one equals three seventy two point four four. What have you gotten into, now? How am I connected to this shit?"

"Relio and company."

"I figured *that*! Big Bad-ass John! What else?"

"That's what we're investigating. I guess they want to shut you up, because they told the gringa there was a really old dude in Gualaca who would tell her they were good, honest, sincere, upright, religious people to deal with. She told me, I told her about you. She was being followed by John. She got off the bus, here, to make them think she was going to see you. John followed her. She came to the police, and pointed him out. He was heard saying it was some kind of trap, on the phone. You were in the mountains. I guess they wanted to be damned sure she didn't talk to you. They think, or have guessed, Amanda will work with Tero and the corruption board, taking control away from the old crowd at the judicial.

"That about cover it?"

"A lot more than I care to know. How's Tyna? Your brats are making a name for themselves."

They chatted awhile. The call from the registro came in. It was, indeed, the same crowd who were setting up something with George and Ethan. The Bocas property was under the name of one of the crook's wife, stolen from a retired gringo who had gone back to the states, dead broke. The land here was owned by a development company- who were selling it with corporate papers. The company was based in Colombia and Mexico.

Dave heard that. "DUH! I don't know what property you're talking about, but it will be the perfect place to set up a lavanderia, complete with a hotel and casino! It would take in millions a day! In cash! They would have to make daily deposits of all that spanking clean cash!!

"I'm going to Buabidi for a couple of weeks. Get this shit settled before I get back! That's an order!"

Clint and Tero gave him the bird.

"Well, I think I have a place to look," Clint said. "I haven't used a disguise in fifteen years! This should be fun. I wonder if I can pull it off against that crowd, though it's been as long since I saw any of them, face-to-face."

"As you told Mrs. Presley, on several occasions, be very damned careful!"

The sour old man got off the Bocas bus in Almirante. The handsome Indio who most people there had seen around quite a lot got his bags from the bus, and hailed a taxi to have them delivered to the water taxi for Isla Colón. They got to the taxi, and Obilio presented the old man's passport and paid for their tickets.

"Amos Aztric Aaron. Seventy eight years old. Portland, Oregon. Tourist visa. Possibly an investor," Filomena, the girl selling the tickets said, as she flirted with Obilio, Obilio made damned certain certain that hangers-around heard that.

"He's not easy to work for," Obilio replied. "He pays damned well! Got money up the ass.

"Actually, he's not so bad, once you get to know him. It's mostly an act so the local beggars and scam artists will stay clear of him. I can tell he's got a few million he wants to move down here. I heard him call 'unreported funds' when he was talking with that Contini hood, in Chiriqui Grande – that fat Colombian everybody knows is a transfer man for the cartels – like he'd give a shit about a pequeño couple of million ... I better get him on the boat. See you later!"

"Toward the back!" Amos snapped. "It's choppy. Smoother ride in back. Let the broads sit up front and squeal when we hit the waves. Stupid! Think it's cute. Think we gringos don't know they've been across a hundred times when it's really rough. Stupid games people play. They don't fool *me*!"

"What the hell?" Obilio said, shrugging. "We get the good seats, they get to be cute."

"You, I like! Think like I do. Those tamale things you got in Almirante were good. Not greasy like too much here.

"You said you're from Bocas? You know anybody with a good deal on some land? I might want a sort of winter place, down here. Oregon's pure hell, in the winter. Be nice to lay around on my own beach house in the tropics. Earned it! Busted my ass for sixty years! I've earned a little rest and R and R. Heard there are some wild chicas here!

"Learned a trick from a friend. Old fart my age. Looks like he'll keel over, any minute. Tells them he has a will that leaves a million dollars to whoever he's with when he croaks. They try to kill him with sex!

"Beautiful area. You're from Bocas?"

"Isla San Cristóbal. It's the big island to our

right, after we get into the bay. I think there are a couple of places for sale, there. I know some people. Maybe I can find you a deal, if you like the island."

As they passed the island, Amos said to have the boat drop them off, there. He'd see if it was the kind of place he would like. Or especially liked. He liked it, already, from a distance. Obilio said that boat didn't go to the island. They could rent a boat and go to all the islands. Tomorrow.

As they disembarked in Bocas Town, a black man, about seventy years old, came to hand Amos a card:

Relio Izquierdo
Call me Lardo
Everybody does
I find whatever you seek
Cel - 6999-0000

Obilio nodded, slightly, at Amos when Lardo was oggling a pretty girl who walked past. Amos smirked.

"Do you have reservations here?" Lardo asked, in perfect English.

"Yeah, but when you're as tired as I am, you throw caution to the wind," Amos replied. "Actually, Bilio has some place I can stay. With his aunt. Save a bundle – not that I need to save anything."

"Any help you need finding *anything*, call me! It's what I do! I've been doing this sort of thing ever since Noriega got dumped, and I found myself out of work. I was with him a lot, you know."

"You got connections for getting a few things? Like investment things?" Amos demanded.

"Uh, Amos. Don't talk about that kind of thing in places like this. You don't know who's a crook, or who's government, two types you don't care to have hear you," Obilio warned. "We could meet for dinner, somewhere, and talk about that kind of thing." He winked at Lardo, who said that was a good idea. After all, even *he* was just some guy on a dock! He nodded at Obilio, and grinned.

"Yeah. Shut me up when I get too stupid," Amos said. "Where's a good restaurant? We can clean up, rest, and meet at, oh, seven, there. Talk about the weather and women and stuff."

"Nine degrees?" Obilio asked.

"Overpriced, so-so service. The food's okay, but why not the Pirate or Toro?"

"Too noisy. The Reef or ... Refugios?"

"How about The Lemon Grass?" Lardo suggested. "Maybe our friend would prefer more native food? Out by the cemetery. Julia's. Best chicken you ever tasted!"

"I've heard about that one. Would you like

some very good Panamanian food?"

"Yeah. I'm getting sick of fancy shit. I'm more basic. Give me, what do you call it? Pollo aguisado? I had that stuff in Santiago. Delicious, and only two bucks!"

"Everything costs more, here. It's three fifty," Lardo said, with a laugh.

"And the other places it's fifteen bucks. Seven sharp, or I eat without you.

"Oh! I'm Amos. Call me AA."

They waved, and started on. Lardo called to Obilio, who went to say a few words, then returned.

"Wants to make a deal with me. Thousands. I mentioned all those restaurants because he's not allowed inside the door at any of them."

Amos (Clint) nodded. They went to Obilio's aunt's house, and he got a room assigned to him. Only Indios could stay there. Clint was declared Ngobe, long ago. He and Obilio made some plans. Clint called Tero, who would have the corruption board waiting.

They were heading for Julia's when, of all people, Amanda came by. That could screw up this thing! Big time!

She waved, and asked if he was new on the island.

"Just got here, two hours ago. Kind of like it here. Might stay. Might buy a place."

"Don't! Don't get involved with land, here! You'll lose your ass!?

"So I've heard. Saw some of it. Know most of the scams. I ain't no raw tourist who don't know his ass from a cow turd! Got to watch your back in these places!"

He was glad his disguises were so good. She didn't even suspect him. They chatted a minute, then Obilio said they had a dinner date, and it was almost time. He was always prompt, unlike the culture, here. They parted, with Clint saying he would probably see her around the town, tomorrow. She said she was going to Changuinola, tomorrow, then to Chiriqui Grande. Clint said they stopped in Chiriqui Grande. It was nice, but there was nothing there. He'd heard Changuinola was just a typical, loud, typical burg.

They went on to meet Lardo at Julia's.

They had a truly delicious meal. They talked about the local area. Amos said he sort of liked David. And Santiago. He would probably prefer the Caribbean to the Pacific, though. He liked being around the ocean, not in it. He might like to own a winter house here, if he could find a deal. He knew land on the islands was expensive, but still a third of what the same thing would cost in the states. Here, he could enjoy a lot of things, being near the water. In Oregon it was all for the view. You didn't actually go *in* the water!

Well, it rained all the time, for part of the year, so you were in it, in that sense, ha-ha.

"I know about a couple of places on San Cristóbal, if you don't insist on being on this island," Lardo replied, giving Obilio a look. "Bilio will know about some of them, I'll know about some. Maybe there's something there to your taste. There are places here, but the price is ridiculous."

"*That's* more to *my* taste! Trouble is, she's maybe twenty, and I'm maybe eighty!"

"Nita? She's nineteen," Obilio said. "You'll find the young girls here like mature men."

"I'm not mature. I'm old. They like old farts, anywhere – so long as the old fart has a lot of money!"

"You've got a lot of money," Bilio pointed out.

"But not a lot of stamina. I guess there's always those hard-on things."

"Well, there are always women, here," Lardo said. "Do you think you would be interested in a small place, or a larger one, where you could have privacy?"

"You can get any of those things at the farmacia. You probably don't need a prescription, seeing you're a gringo."

"How much do you want to spend?" Lardo asked, stubbornly.

"Spend? What do they cost, here? You get a pretty good one, in David, for about twenty five or thirty dollars, but they'll be more here. Tourist trap."

"Twenty five or thirty? Pretty good? What...?"

"Women. What the hell were we talking about?" Amos snapped.

"I was talking about land."

"Oh. No more than two million. A place that's big enough for, as you said, privacy. I don't know if I'll like it that much, yet. We can go tomorrow. Obilio said he knows of a place or two."

"I can get you a better deal than most. I know the people, and they trust me to see they don't get screwed. (Obilio hid a sharp laugh behind a coughing fit. He indicated he's got something caught in his throat). I will be honest. I won't allow anyone to take advantage of my friends. That's why they'll sell through me at half what they'll sell through the usual crooked realtors here.

"You can *not* trust a realtor in Panamá!"

"You can *not* trust a realtor anywhere in the world. Realtors and lawyers. And politicians. No matter where, they're the exact same. Particularly developers. Bunch of cheap, slimy, asshole crooks to the last one!"

Obilio hid another laugh. Lardo had said he held a realtor's license. (Which Clint knew he didn't.)

"Uh! Yes! That's why I don't practice it, though I got a licnese. I was disgusted with that whole bunch!"

"Well, let's say, tomorrow morning, early, we go over there to look around. Who knows? I sort of liked what I saw, on the way over here. On the boat."

"Fine! I'll see you around ... eight? Eight thirty?"

"I said early, not mid-morning! How about five?"

"Five thirty. Guillermo?" Obilio suggested.

"Uh, good enough!"

Later, Obilio said Lardo was never up before nine. He'd suggested eight, because that wouldn't be too early to stick it out for a bundle.

"I know," Clint replied. "That's why I suggested five."

They did a high five.

Lardo looked like he would fall asleep on his feet, but he was at the dock at five thirty. Guillermo had a return, then. He brought workers over at five, and went back at five forty. They got on the clean boat. Guillermo raised an eyebrow when Lardo got on board with them. Bilio grinned, and winked at him.

It was very calm, on the trip over. The breeze was just beginning when they got off on the island. The dock, such as it was, was a few boards on a pair of log uprights

Clint asked if that would support Lardo's weight. Guillermo said they loaded cows from it, so it probably would. Lardo didn't weigh too much more than a cow. He said it in an innocent way, but you could easily tell he didn't like Lardo. Bilio said they would start on the property on the ridge, which Miguel owned, and would sell, if he was in one of the periods when he was desperate for cash.

"Why not start at Nica's, just out of town?" Lardo asked, quickly.

"Nica's in David. We can't argue with him," Bilio answered.

"Oh, I have an authority to show his property."

"Like shit!" Clint heard Guillermo say, just behind him.

"It's no difference to me," Clint said. "I'll have to see everything that's available before I decide on anything. I do like this island!"

"Nica's my brother. He doesn't want to sell anything. He wouldn't let that fat pig on his land, if he did," Guillermo said – in Ngobere. Lardo had always refused to learn the dialect. Clint spoke it, almost as his first language, anymore, but Amos wouldn't understand a word of it.

"What? Speak Spanish when there are people around who don't speak dialect!" Lardo demanded, in Spanish.

"In case it slipped by you, we only speak English around Amos. He doesn't speak much Spanish," Bilio returned, in English. "Guillermo just said he didn't think *his brother*, Nica, wanted to sell that part."

"Well, you said there was a place on the top of a mountain that was over the water, high enough to where you could see all over the Caribbean and Isla Colón. Some Miguel owns it, and you know he wants to sell. It sounds like what I'd like."

"You have to climb a big damned mountain to get there!" Lardo wailed.

"Good way to help guarantee privacy. Let's look at that, and at the others on the way back down."

"But you have to go over that mountain, right there, cross the valley, and climb to that part!"

"No problem! Oregon has mountains a lot worse than that. We argue all day, we don't see nothing! We can all use some exercise – well, you and me. Guillermo won't be with us, I suppose. Bilio is in better shape than I ever was, in my life, and I was in pretty damned good shape. At one time." He waved to go on. Obilio grinned, and winked at Guillermo, as Clint followed him to the trail.

"Could we get a drink at the tienda before we start our ten mile hike?" Lardo asked, sourly.

"There's water, several places, but we can take some chicha, I suppose," Bilio answered. "We'll be back here at, say, four?"

"Heee! That's eight hours!" Lardo whined.

"You don't have to go. You invited yourself," Clint said, with a suspicious look at him.

"Oh! I'm not serious! I didn't have my second cup of coffee, this morning, so I tend to be an ass. Lead on, Hanibal!"

"Hanibal had to tend bar, last night. He isn't here. Obilio can show you everything he could," Guillermo said, innocently.

Lardo didn't fall for it. Obilio said, "Four!"

and turned to lead along a rocky path to the left. It went along the soccer field, and turned into a trail among cacao trees.

"This is the main way to get there, from this side. You can go directly up the other side, if you build a small dock. Miguel will give rights of passage, of course. He wouldn't expect anyone living on that side to use this trail, all the time."

"This place is beautiful!" Clint exclaimed. "It looks just like the pictures you showed me! I really expected they would be carefully arranged to show off the best parts, but it's everywhere you look!"

"Wait until you see the property!" Bilio said. "This is just ordinary land – for here. You have a view from the top, plus all this."

"Is there chocolate there, like this?"

"Cacao, yuca, pineapples, bananas, coconuts, pifas, mormones, cashews, guayaba, guanabana, you name it. It's all native, here."

"Wow! How many acres did you say he had?"

"I didn't say acres. Hectares."

"Hectares are as big as acres?"

"Bigger," Lardo answered. "People come from the United States, and think the price asked is a little high, sometimes, but they're thinking in acres.

"When I tell them it's thirty thousand a

hectare, they think I mean acres, and usually say it's about a fourth higher than they thought land sold for, here. Some friend got a place on the island for just twenty five an acre. It was worth it, there – well, they all say it's worth it, here, but they have budgets that won't allow that. When they learn it's less than ten thousand an acre, they can't believe it!

"I have four places sold, here, for more than Miguel wants. Everyone knows they got a deal that only comes along once in life!"

They came to the top of the first mountain, in about an hour. Clint had been there, dozens of times. He gushed, "God! It's everything you said, except ... where's the Caribbean?"

"This is part of Miguel's land. That peak over there is the property I told you about. You'll think this was dull, when you see that one!"

Lardo was puffing up the rough path, about fifty feet below. Clint grinned, and said to be sure the recorder and transmitter were working, then louder, as he excitedly talked about the land.

"Say! That Elvis woman said she was buying something out here. You remember her? The woman in Chiriqui Grande?"

"Elvis? That's not a woman's name. You ... Oh! You mean Mrs. Presley! I think she was looking at a place on the tip, out that way." He pointed.

Clint winked at Obilio. Lardo was whining that he had to sit, for a few minutes. Amos was right, when he said they were out of shape! Maybe Amos had seen enough that he could picture ... he'd seen the pictures! He saw that everything was exactly the same as the photos! There really wasn't any reason to go all that distance!"

"You said this Miguel person was ready to sell fifty hectares for two point two million? That we could probably get him down to one eight?

"I want to see that place! If this is part of it, and that place is like the pictures, to hell with arguing about it!"

"Er, Bilio? Can I speak with you – in private?" Lardo said, with a wink at Obilio, then to Clint. "Uh, Amos, there is a disparity in the prices we were told. I thought we were talking about two point four million. It seems the Indios stick together. There's not much use in me going up there, if Bilio can get it that much cheaper!"

"No problem! I want to go over by that stream! It looks like one of those paradise places on TV! My God!"

Clint went, almost running, to the little sparkling creek, to stare in the water, and yell that one of those fancy fish, just like there were dozens of in that stream, sold for eighty bucks, in the states!

He turned on his radio to listen.

L: "You really are going for two when Miguel will sell it for one two fifty – and he's biting! We have to make a deal! We can get it all! All we have to do is get Miguel's signature on a traspas, and this mark's signature on a promisory! I know a notario who'll stamp it! We can go through the registro, and end up with the money *and* the property!"

O: "No. I won't screw Miguel, that way. I'll make what I can on the deal. I would let Amos argue it down to a million seven fifty, but I'm not out to screw my own people!"

L: "Don't screw this up! I've worked all my life to get something that gets me something, not just those mafia character who just use me!"

O: "We can sell it for two two fifty, and you and I each get a half million. Everybody's happy with the deal, and it's totally legal."

L: "But we could get a lot more!"

O: "I don't want a lot more. I don't want any more. What would I do with it?"

L: "No! We can get more! I won't let you screw me out of this!"

O: "What in hell are you talking about? You're just along! You're aren't included, in it! I was going to let you make a little, but about two more words, and you can take a fucking hike! I will *not* screw my people! I do *not* want to screw anyone!"

L: "We'll just see! You'll find I know people!"

O: "Like the ones who you just said used you and you ended up on the streets, working silly little petty scams on tourists? When you could get half a million, legally?

"What do you mean, you have a notario who will stamp the papers for us?"

L; "For me! For the people I work for, sometimes! Not for you! You're not going to go to him and get it all! It's part mine!"

O: "Okay. Let's finish with Amosm and go back. I'll see whether you have a notarym or whether you're trying to con me! If you are, get ready to be crab bait!" He turnedm and called, "Amos? Ready to go on?"

"Yeah! This place is really fantastic!" Clint came back, and looked expectantly at Obilio.

"It seems I had almost promised the land to a Mr. Smith, from the United States, for two point three, "Lardo said. "Bilio says he has first choice on the land, but I'm sure Miguel will want all he can get.

"How about we split the difference?"

"What difference? Fifty lousy thousand dollars? Maybe I can offer two three, and no one can object? I love this place!

"I have to see from that mountain! Let's go!"

"I'll call Guillermo. Maybe he'll be able to

pick us up on that side. It'll save us having to cross back across this mountain," Obilio suggested. Clint shrugged, and forged ahead.

When they reached the second peak, they had to wait more than twenty minutes for Lardo to catch up. He looked like he would have a heart attack, any second.

Clint laughed. "I decided we can go back the way we came! I'm not tired, in the least. I'd like to see it all, again!"

"Oh, no! Please!" Lardo wailed. "I can't! I just ... can't!" He sat on a log, and was actually crying.

"Just joking. Guillermo will pick us up in half an hour, this side. It's all downhill, from here.

"You really shouldn't let yourself get so sloppied up! I think you'd probably drop dead if we really did have to walk back!"

Lardo tried to grin. "You're right about that!"

Clint and Obilio would meet with Lardo, in the morning, at ten, to go to a notary. Clint said five thirty, but the notary didn't open until nine thirty, and had an appointment, then.

He had a wire, as did Obilio. Tero had a man and woman from Panamá City in the Ministerio offices beside the notary. Obilio said the notary wasn't usually open Tuesdays, but a "special" notario was there, on the island, and would handle things on the official side. Lardo said he already had a certificado from Miguel to present.

Miguel was a good friend of Clint's. Clint knew perfectly damned well there was no such paper. These same people had tried to con him out of his land, three times. One time, they tried to kill him before he could claim the papers were false. They had missed, if just barely. Clint had called, and told him what they were doing, as soon as they got back from his property. He would, hopefully, lay low until it was finished. This time, they might really be able to kill him. It was an old game, here. Get false papers, then kill the Indio, and there was no one left to contest the papers. The trouble would be, for Clint, keeping Miguel from charging in and making it easy for them to get rid of him.

They could tag the corrupt notary. Maybe they could get one or more of the others, with this. If they could get enough on this one, Amanda's testimony, and the fact they couldn't get around the added fact they were the only possible suspects in her ex-husband's and her brother's murders, would tie it. Maybe it would bring a few other crooked deals of the type to light. Once the anti-corruption board found themselves in a position where they were forced to act, things could get serious. Fast!

They sat in Chitres, and had some good coffee and hojaldres, then went to the notary, Wilyam Sorroco, the notary, met them outside the front door, and said the fumigators had come. They could handle everything in the Pirate, if that was suitable. Lardo said it didn't matter where, just so long as they got it done before Amos changed his mind!

"Oh, I won't change my mind on this one, I guarantee! I intend to get this done so I can start my other projects!"

They went to the Pirate, as suggested. There was a woman, there, that Lardo greeted like he was surprised to see her! She could help them, because they needed a witness who wasn't in on the business. They had planned to use a waitress, but she was there, so what the hell?

Clint noticed that they had worded the contract to say she was a majority partner with Lardo and a person in David. The major person Amanda was supposed to deal with. *What* a *coincidence*!

The contracts were in Spanish. Clint saw that Amos, who didn't, so far as they knew, speak five words in Spanish, read and understood Spanish perfectly.

"I ain't signing any contract that I can't read!" Clint cried.

"I have an English translation, right here," Lardo said. "Obilio can read them both, and tell you they say the same thing."

"I don't read much English. I just speak it, from working with the tourists," Obilio, who read English as well as he spoke it, said. He had claimed he couldn't, to Lardo, yesterday.

The woman, Lila Loranzo, picked them up, read for a couple of minutes, and said, "Well, other than when you said the shore, orilla, with Rauz was the south border, instead of borden, the border, they say the same thing. Does that make a difference, legally?"

"No. Shore or border is the same term, legally," the notario, Jesus Flores, said. "I have an appointment, in Almirante. I will have to hurry. Please?”

"Well, okay,” Amos answered. “You aren’t part of the deal, so you wouldn’t have anything to gain by lying.” He signed the contract, *Amos A. Aaron,* and handed Lardo a certified bank check for two million three hundred thousand dollars, made out to Miguel Abrego Juarez Jaramilio.

"But..!!” Lardo exclaimed. “This is made out to Juarez, not me! Where did you get his full name from? I mean ... I didn’t know the Jaramilio part, uh.”

"What? Of course! You said it was his property you were selling. Why would I give you the money? It’s up to him to pay the commissions and so forth, isn’t it, Obilio?

"It’s his name, just like that, on the plan you gave me. Naturally, it’s in his name!”

"Er? The plano? Er?” He was sweating. Profusly.

"What’s going on here!? Why in hell did you think I’d hand you two million dollars? Are you out of your mind, or just stupid?”

Three people came in the door, and headed for their table. Lardo looked like he’d faint. Loranzo suddenly stood, and said she had to go, but the woman coming to the table said she was under arrest. Sit down!

"Hi, Miguel. I thought you promised not to get

involved in this. What? You're suicidal?" Obilio said.

"When there's a check for two million dollars here, for me?

"Hi, Obilio. I thought you said Clint would be here. Tell him I said thanks for the money. I really need it. You can tell him Manny will see it's used in the foundation's work, and that I know I'm to give a million of it back. I can do that.

"Oh, yes! This is Irena Villardes and Samy Arends. They're with the corruption board. We were listening to all of this, outside. Those papers, there, will put the bunch of you in the penitentiary, where you belong!

"Obilio did explain to you that the check was to catch this bunch of crooks?"

"Yeah. I didn't ever know what was going on. I really do want to buy some of that land."

"It belongs to the foundation, now. I don't know if they would sell a part of it."

"This Clint character is that guy we met in Chiriqui Grande? The gringo you said was an Indio?" Clint asked.

"Yes. He was on his way back to the comarca. He has a nice place, there. In Cusapín," Obilio answered. "He's the one who had me set this up with you."

Lardo groaned, and swore. "They'll kill me for

this! Not *Faraday*! Oh, god!"

"If there's one person in Bocas Province who has no right to call on god, it's you!" Miguel snarled.

Sorroco said he had to use the facilities, and stood. Arends grinned, and shrugged. Three minutes later, a policeman came in the front, with Sorroco. "Not exactly original," The policeman said. He shoved Sorroco, not too gently, into his seat.

They all signed reports, and Irena collected all the papers. Miguel went with Wilyam to the internet café to have a lot of copies of the check made. Three and a half hours later, Clint headed for the water taxi, to return to David. Amos got on the bus, and rode to Chiriqui Grande. Clint got on the bus, ten minutes later, to ride to David. He called Tyna, then Amanda. He explained what had happened. He said they had the door open to see her ex-husband's killer tagged. Some people who had no explanation for a lot of things were going to have to give explanations. It was going to get dangerous. She was *not* to get involved in this part.

"I've learned, through a very clever investigation, that my ex, good old George, and my dear *dear* brother, were working with those people to get me to give them a few hundred thousand dollars for some land they didn't own.

The owners are on a year-long vacation to Spain. They were about to find themselves in a position where I would find out. Tero's saving it for the other thing you're doing. He said it will add up only one way, so this is like what we would call icing on the cake.

"I think I've about had my fill of excitement. Go for it! Keep me informed, okay?"

"Will do."

"I found a boyfriend, here. One who is really neat, and one I can trust."

"I could see that, coming! Tell Tero I said hi. Tell him what we've done, though he already has some reports."

"What we have to worry about is the corrupt people in the fiscalia. As soon as they hear about what went down in Bocas, they'll report to that bunch of slime. They'll run, probably to Costa Rica," Tero warned.

"We'll cut them off at the pass," Capt. Silvio Bonifero promised. Clint had worked with him in Santiago and in Las Tablas. He was as strong as Tero about getting rid of the corruption in the Panamanian police and court system.

"We'll have a bit of a problem proving they were the only ones who could have killed Amanda's ex and her brother, but I think, considering the charges from Bocas, we can swing it," Clint replied.

"I found a solid witness who saw one of them nearby in Big Badass John's car. They waited at that restaurant, just before the cutoff to Bugaba. They almost ran out when a black SUV of some type went in, then came back, five minutes later with another person in the car with them," Tero said. "John has a problem when there's a goodlooking chica around. He gets mouth flutters, so gets attention. They notice things, after that. This time the fiscalia isn't going to misplace their testigo forms, I'll guarantee. They have a real problem, because the corruption board has the major witnesses and the arrestees going directly to Panamá City, not to Changuinola or David. As soon as they get that little bit of news, several here are going to run for cover."

"There's noplace they can go. I found out about the way to Costa Rica, out past Puerto Armuelles, and they won't dare to try Rio Sereno – not that they'll get that far," Silvio said. "This isn't the worst coffee I've ever tasted, but it's way up there!"

They sat around and chatted until Tero's friend at the fiscalia said the news about Lardo and company was just then coming in. It was being given to the news media, very quickly, to stop attempts to silence or cover.

"Now it gets interesting!" Clint said. "I sort of wish I wasn't too old to go after a few of them, personally!"

"You've already done a hell of a lot more than your duty," Silvio replied.

Amanda came in. They watched the news together.

"... was not expected to get to the point of excess violence, but the person described only as 'John' drew a pistol from under the seat, and shot at Officer Torres, who suffered a wound in the left arm. John was hit with no less than twenty four shots. Officer Lariez stated, loudly, that these thugs and hoods had better understand that there was no longer anyone to protect them, and noplace to go. They would be insane to continue fighting arrest. Officer Jolandero, who fired first at John when John shot Officer Torres, said the old thing from the EE. UU. known as zero tolerance was in effect.

"We will inform you as quickly as new facts become known."

"Jolandero! He's as corrupt as anyone there!" Tero cried.

"And he's in a position to see that the ones who can testify against him don't live long enough to do it, isn't he?" Amanada asked.

"Let him save the Panamanian people a few million dollars, then tag his ass," Silvio suggested. They all agreed on that point!

A few minutes later: "This just coming in! The officer, Jolandero, who earlier led a team against a group of killers and thugs has just been shot! He was going into a house where three of the persons sought for ... what?

"It seems there was a firefight. Jolandero was caught between. There is a question ... yes. There is a question of whether he was shot with friendly fire or ... what? None at all? ... The house was entered. There were no weapons found, inside. There was no firing from the house that anyone can say ... what? He was? I see ... I have just been informed that Jolandero was under investigation as being a part of the ... yes? ... that the one, John, who he led the attack against, had been seen with him, on several occasions, that there is video evidence of three such meetings, taken by the corruption board in an earlier criminal investigation. Another officer in the team where Jolandero was shot is also under investigation. Our own reporter at the scene says we have a video that shows, definitely, that Officer Williams deliberately shot Jolandero. Williams is, even at this very moment, en route to the house of Judge Penchante. There will be someone there to thwart his getting to the judge, who also is, and has been, the subject of investigations.

"All we can do is wait.

"Well, Yolanda! It seems this is going to be one of those things like when the people rose up against the same thing, a few months ... yes? Very well. To our reporter at the home of Judge Penchante. It seems Williams is surrounded, and refuses to submit to arrest."

"It is a stand-off, at the moment. I'm Roberto Morales, reporting from the home of Judge Penchante.

"Officer Williams is in a car, and is holding a fellow officer, Sara Menendez, at gunpoint, and is threatening to kill her if he is not allowed to leave. He has an AK forty seven and his sidearm. There are several officers surrounding the car, at a distance, and (sharp sound of a single shot) ... wait a moment. Did you get that on video, Eduardo?

"A trained Action Team sniper has just shot Williams. Officer Menendez is unharmed. It will take a moment to untangle this. Back to you, Yolanda."

Amanda turned the sound down. "It's all over, except the excuses," she said.

"That won't work, anymore," Silvio replied.

"So. What's for dinner? I want to get back to my wife!" Clint said.

"Well, you managed to clean that rats nest out!" Amanda said.

"Oh, come down to Earth!" Silvio demanded. "We got a few on the edges. The main core is still there."

That, sadly, is the way of the world, anymore.

Clint leaned back and smiled at Tyna, who teased at him.

He was in a hammock on his porch, facing the calm Caribbean. He had just come back from making a frijole bed for the village. They would have enough for the area, from this. Maybe they would sell some to buy flour and such.

Matilde, the local medicine woman, came by to wave and ask how things were.

"Tranquil," Tyna called back.

That was also the way of the world, albeit a very different world from only a few kilometers away.

C. D. Moulton's works are available on most major outlets as printed or e-books. CD writes the CD Grimes, PI, mysteries, the Det. Lt. Nick Storie mysteries, the Clint Faraday mysteries, the Flight of the Maita science fiction series, books on orchid culture and many others of many types. Mystery, adventure, intrigue, science fiction, humor, fantasy, paranormal, mild erotica, and factual.